THRILLS 'N' CHILLS

An anthology of short stories and poetry from the Avalon Writing Group

To Lydia,

I love your work!
Hope you enjoy
'Thrills 'n' Chills'.

Victoria Wat

A Wild Wolf Publication

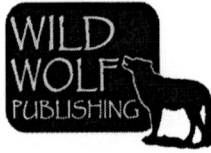

WILD
WOLF
PUBLISHING

Published by Wild Wolf Publishing in 2014

Copyright © 2014 Avalon Writing Group

First print

ISBN: 978-1-907954-40-5

Also available in e-book

www.wildwolfpublishing.com

In September 2012, I began a weekly Creative Writing group at Di Meo's Delaval Ices in Whitley Bay, North Tyneside. For the first few weeks, one person attended. Then another one started to come regularly. By January 2013, the group was averaging about five or six people a week. In September 2013, I began a second group at Quilliam Brothers Teahouse in Newcastle.

The writers who attend the groups write poetry, script, prose and Creative Non-Fiction. Some are absolute beginners, others have been writing for a long time. In the sessions, we use different writing exercises to inspire their writing. I may give an opening line or a picture prompt, perhaps ask the group to do a small treasure hunt. No matter which task I set, they always come up with some exciting and unique writing. I feel so privileged to work with these fantastic writers on a regular basis and truly enjoy seeing them experiment and hone their craft.

Members of both groups have contributed to three performance evenings which have been tremendously well-received. This anthology contains several pieces that were first performed at The Avalon, Whitley Bay, in November 2013.

As I'm sure you will agree, this collection is just the beginning for many of the writers featured.

Victoria Watson

Road Kill

By Jean Laurie

Jean Laurie is inspired to write when an event in the physical world resonates with an emotional experience. She has had several poems and short stories included in anthologies, so she hopes that readers share that emotional response.

I hate driving the A597 on moonless nights. The bends and dips in the old road make it difficult to drive at any speed. I'm a fast driver - too fast, my wife says - but I want to get home. Don't get me wrong, I love my job, but the worst part of it is the monthly meetings in London to discuss sales figures and key performance indicators. I've pointed out all that stuff could be done by Skype but Darren, my boss, says we can't do the motivational team building stuff unless we're together. All that high fiving and management speak leaves me cold. Just let me get on with it I think. I'm good at my job, driving all over the country chasing gremlins out of computer systems.

I've only ever had one accident in all those years of driving. Not counting the rabbits that freeze in the headlights, the odd fox and pheasant. They don't count, they don't leave any dents in the bodywork. But just along this road I hit a deer. One of the wild ones that graze all over the fells. It just ran out of a coppice of trees as I came round the bend. Thought of stopping and taking it home for venison, but I just kept on going. Not worth the bother.

The girl solidified from one of the bands of mist that lie like chiffon scarves in the shallow valleys. My foot's ramming the brake pedal into the floor and my hands are spinning the steering wheel as far to the left as it can go. I felt the car hit the ditch and the tree trunk loomed closer. When I come to, there's a pain in my shoulder and chest where the seat belt caught me, and a bruised lump on my forehead. The car has tipped into the ditch, the headlights reflecting in the muddy pools at the bottom. Everywhere else is blackness.

At first, I thought the noise was the wind in the trees. But it was a whispering, insistent, menacing hiss in a language I didn't recognise. I pulled my mobile phone from my pocket. It fell into small pieces in my hand. I tried the door handle and pushed the door open as far as it would go. The pain in my shoulder nearly made me pass out again and I retched.

The inside of the ditch nearest the road was higher than my head and sheer mud. After a few attempts to scramble up, I splashed through the pooled water and clambered up the other side. on the edge of the forest. The hissing noise was louder here.

Then she was in front of me, the girl. Long limbed, in a soft brown dress, her face was narrow, with a long nose and huge brown eyes.

'Are you hurt?' I ask. She doesn't reply, just turns me round to face the forest. A herd of deer are standing near us. Leading them is a stag, big as a cow, with a set of magnificent, murderous antlers. He advances on us and I try to move away, but the girl's arms are round me now and she's laughing softly in my ear, throaty and triumphant. The stag lowers his head and gathers speed. I scream as the antler grazes my side, feel blood

6

spurting from just below my ribs. The girl pushes me out of the circling deer, into the woods.

I ran as fast as the twisting tree roots and clutching brambles would allow. I could hear the deer getting closer, felt warm breath on my back. I came upon the fence suddenly and climbed over. The barbed wire tore my hands as I tried to stop my fall on the other side. Terrified, I ran through the barley field, disturbing rabbits and voles, who shot off in all directions.

When the stag caught me, his antlers hoisted me into the air and tossed me across the field. The landing pushed the breath from my lungs. As if they knew I couldn't run any more, they trampled over me. They circled me again. I thought they'd kill me, but they just stared at my broken body. As if satisfied with their work, they rumbled back into the woods.

Now I'm lying in the field, hot with August sunshine. My lips are parched and cracking, but the pain in my broken limbs and body has receded to a stinging numbness. The sky above me is the most beautiful blue. The noise of the combine harvester methodically cutting the corn is mesmerising, coming nearer and nearer. But I can't raise an arm to stop it. Rabbits and voles and field mice are retreating to this final corner of the field to be cut, running past me, some taking refuge under my body. I close my eyes and wait.

The Blackness

By Harry Gallagher

Harry Gallagher has been writing for much of his life and one day soon hopes to join up the letters. Until then he lives in hope on the coast with a very patient daughter and very small dog.

The blackness is here again, Mummy. The lady, she has taken Baby James and me to her tree pen and our feet hurt. James has been crying, but I have stroked his hair like you taught me. I am hungry. And cold.

James is asleep now and the lady is combing his hair with her fingernails. She is rocking. The trees will look after us, won't they? It is dark, but I know we are in the forest because there are twigs and leaves all around us. There is also an owl nearby, too-witting. And another too-wooing.

I hope you can hear me talking to you in my head. The dark lady says no-one can hear us now. I am sorry if I have upset you. The dark lady says that is why we are here. She also says there is no God, but that is not true is it Mummy?

My tummy is rumbling and my throat hurts, but that's not because I want to cry, honestly. I am a brave girl and will look after Baby James.

The dark lady has fallen asleep now. I don't like the dark lady. She is very frightening and I don't like being frightened. But I am very brave and big for my age. But I don't know the way out. Everywhere is covered with twigs and leaves and cobwebs; and the

9

lady says the spiders are all deadly poisonous and little children like me and Baby James would be killed and eaten in five minutes if we tried to run away. I hate her and I want to come home. Please Mummy!

Argh! What was that? It sounds like- argh! Again! It's like a big rock crashing onto- argh! Again! Oh no, it's getting closer! Mummy I want to come home! My head is aching and my chest hurts and James is awake and crying. But the lady is still asleep – why?

James, come here; come to me. Quick, run! Come on James, faster! I know, I know you're only a baby but.....come here, I'll carry you. Faster, faster! Mummy, I can't run quickly enough. My arms hurt from carrying poor James. Ow! My knee, my elbows! James are you alright?

Mummy, please help! We are both crying now and I wish you could hear me in your head. I can't remember what you look like. Everything is fading away...

* * * * * *

I don't know who is there now, or if anyone can hear. We have been here for a long, long time now. We haven't seen the witch lady for.....oh I don't know how long, and I don't believe you are there at all. I don't even know why I talk to you.

There is no way out of this awful place. It is dark all the time and the terrible noise is here every night. The trees groan and moan to us about the end of days. Sometimes it feels like I have lost months, or even years. James looks a lot older than a baby now and I feel older too. I have taught him how to talk, and tell

10

him what you and Daddy taught me – that people are kind and nice. But he doesn't believe me and I don't think I do either.

There is no explanation as to why you have abandoned us. I sometimes think I see you, but that hasn't happened for the longest time. The witch woman told us before she disappeared that I was mad, and that you and Daddy had me put away because I had killed James but I didn't, did I Mummy? And besides, James is right here with me, aren't you James. James…?

Sapitwa

By James Grosvenor

James Grosvenor has a BA (Hons) in History from Newcastle University and normally writes historical fiction, with a particular interest in the late medieval period. He is currently working on a novel set in Northumberland in the years leading up to the beginning of the Wars of the Roses. James is married and has two sons.

Sapitwa, the tallest point of Mount Mulanje, towering over 3,000 metres above the fertile farm land of south Malawi. The highest peak in Central Africa.

Sapitwa. Beautiful, remote, uninhabited.

Sapitwa. The people of the plain whisper the name with reverence, apprehension and foreboding.

Sapitwa. There is a lonely log cabin there which nestles between two out flung spurs of naked rock, behind it looms the peak. It is shelter. Not much more, somewhere to sleep, a place to light a fire.

Sapitwa. The African sun is hot and relentless, but at this height the breeze is gentle and refreshing. The view over the surrounding plains of Chiradzulu is splendid, imposing, magnificent. You see a patchwork of tea plantations, forests of camphor and cedar lie prostrate below you, it's an avian image, an eagle's revelation.

Sapitwa. The darkness comes. The sun, majestic through the day abdicates in the face of coming night.

And does so with unseemly haste, understandable perhaps this close to the equator. But somehow it seems like a capitulation, the sun departs hurriedly, humiliated before light's dread conqueror.

Sapitwa. As night devours the sky, her inky cloak unfolds, flowing across the landscape. The plantations and the forests disappear, lost in the inexorable tsunami of deep obsidian. From secret hollows and fissures in the rocks, remnants of a more ancient, infinite, primordial night, creep forth to welcome their sister, reclaiming the land, their eternal birth right restored.

Sapitwa. The log cabin doesn't feel like shelter now, the meagre artificial light only serves to accentuate the deep oppressive darkness. You tell yourself it's all your imagination, but you can't shake the feeling that the night is suffused with silent malignant intent. You are an island of rationality, surrounded by a nameless sea of superstitious foreboding. Even the moon and the stars stay hidden, their presence unwelcome here on high dread Sapitwa.

The stories you've heard return unbidden to your consciousness. Once again you see the fear in the eyes of those who tell them, hear the portent in their words. They told you tales about the ones who were lost, the ones who walked the forsaken paths and did not return. The fruitless searches for those who were warned but failed to heed. Will you also number among them?

Sapitwa. The cabin door is closed now, the stout wooden bar in its place. But you know you're not safe. Sapitwa darkness still prowls, hungry, insatiable, searching for a way in. You fancy that it may creep under the door, and slither unbidden into your fragile sanctuary, find you there and overpower you, consume you, devour you.

Is this the fate of the others? Is this where they've gone? Lost forever on Sapitwa? Did they discover that 2000 years of rationalisation is no protection against eternal elemental evil? The young Dutch girl was the last one to go. Did she run out into the darkness? Did she feel the soft heavy velvet embrace of the night? Nobody knows. They spent weeks searching, tracker dogs, mountain guides. Her brother, who gave up his job and wandered the mountain for six months, endured beyond the point where all rational hope had failed. In the end he longed to find a body, or even a shred of his sister's existence. He went home at last, broken, crushed, defeated, another victim of the nameless menace of Sapitwa.

The candles have gone now, you don't know how long it's been. The shadows have enveloped you, you've breathed the cloying darkness. When you opened your mouth in that silent scream, it poured unbidden down your throat. Your wide eyed terror at last betrayed you, the gateway to you soul. It suffuses you, possess you.

You are one with the darkness now. This is where you dwell. You've always been here, haven't you? Here with so many others. This is where you'll stay, forever on bleak Sapitwa.

Sapitwa in the local dialect means simply 'do not go there'. Now you understand why, perhaps you always did?

The Rescue

By Annie Bates

Annie Bates is a retired probation officer, avid reader and frustrating writer.

Graham Turner made a third attempt to attach the cockpit to the body of the Fisler Storck but the piece of grey plastic slipped out of his hand and fell, glue side down, on to the stained maroon cord carpet. He swore softly and grunted as he tried to bend over to pick it up. Years of an increasingly fatty diet had begun to threaten all but the most basic of body movements.

This would not do at all. It was 11 a.m. on a Saturday morning and already he was frustrated and restless. The weekend stretched before him, bleak and unforgiving. He had thought, through an alcohol-hazed Friday night, that he had got it sorted out. He would pass the empty days following his hobbies and small DIY projects in the flat. When he woke up unforgivably early on Saturday morning, the dreariness of the flat seemed to mock him, as did his adolescent love of airfix kits. What was the point of any of it? Kate and the children were 300 miles away enjoying a new life and, presumably, a fulfilling weekend. They, or Kate at least, would not be thinking about him. Laura would doubtless have a riding lesson. Paul would, perhaps, be continuing with his Judo or something similar. There would be parties, D.V.D.s, outings to the shops. All the banalities of family life that had exasperated him so much but which now seemed the very stuff of life.

Deep in self pity, Graham heaved himself out of his chair and stood on his precious piece of plastic. That was it, he would have to go out or he would be in danger of wrecking the flat. He had not yet managed to remedy all the destruction he had caused when he last lost his temper. He peered through the grimy window assessing the weather. As the Look North reporter had said, it was windy with squalls of rain. From where he stood he could just see the waves of the North Sea between the opposite roof tops. The spume threatened to deluge the pavement. He could just make out the inevitable prat showing off, daring the waves like Canute. It would serve him right if he got carried away, good riddance, thought Graham bitterly.

The only trousers that really fitted Graham now were his fleecy jogging bottoms. He wore these, a jolly Christmas jumper his mum had sent him, a fleece and his dreadful old trainers. He knew he looked grim, 45 years old, 6 ft tall, a large head and nose, receding mousy hair and a stomach distended by cheap food and alcohol. His face was now set in a permanent scowl, lines pulling downwards at the sides of his mouth. He believed his ears had grown bigger as his hair had disappeared. He left the dismal reflection in the mirror and stomped downstairs hoping to disturb the other tenants who had been successful in their lie ins.

When he emerged from the gloom of the hallway on to the street, he checked his change. The warehouse paid minimum wage and Graham was constantly short of money. Now in his old job … it didn't do to think about that. At least he was working. He had promised himself he wouldn't go to the Cashpoint until Monday, knowing how little he had for the rest of the month. He

18

looked at the money in his palm hopefully, £3.60, worse than he thought. He sighed miserably. He had no friends locally. From Kent originally, he had moved to the North East for university then work and marriage. His ex had taken the children to live near her parents when they divorced marooning him in this godforsaken place. He supposed he could have moved but he did not have the financial resources or acceptable employment history (but that was another story) to leave. Despite living in the area for twenty odd years, he had never 'got' the accent or the humour. He felt alien and believed himself the butt of jokes although there was scant foundation for this belief.

Thrusting his hands in his pockets he trudged, head down, along the road to the sea front and was hit forcibly by the wind raising spray from the huge waves. Gasping, he attempted to quicken his pace conceding that he would have to find warmth and shelter sooner rather than later.

Skelton Bay had suffered the devastation left by the failure of successive councils to invest in its infrastructure. Additionally, speculators had bought seafront properties only to fail in applications for development or see their money dwindle in the recession. The properties facing the sea, therefore, boasted abandoned half built flats, desolate clubs, a beautiful thirties' cinema closed and sprayed with graffiti and adorned by special brew cans, cider bottles and used condoms. There was a distinct lack of cafes or pubs. If he past this mayhem, however, Graham knew there were signs of a regeneration. Facing the next bay were a chippie, a restaurant and a bar which served food. £3.60 was not going to stretch far but Graham needed the warmth and, who knows, a conversation with someone like-minded.

Graham entered the Sea Horse gratefully. It was all gleaming chrome and polished wood. He peered through the window before entering. It was full of happy families, trendy couples and expensively-dressed kids of all ages. He suddenly baulked at the thought of entering this alien environment but another gust of wind mixed with hail, made up his mind for him. He pushed the door open and was greeted by a wall of conversation and a mixture of enticing smells: chips, soup, fish and beer. His stomach lurched. He regretted his decision to avoid the cash point, leaving his debit card at home to forestall temptation.

Aware that he was standing in the way of people, he made his way to the only free seat he could see. It was detached, evidently parted from its table. It was high-backed boasting a red leather cover punctured by evenly spaced buttons … hideous, he thought. He sat down heavily surveying the bar which was packed with customers three people deep. He decided to delay his order until the crowd died down and began to observe the clientele instead. No one had forbidden him to go to a bar and 'look' had they? Envy rose within him as he stared at the smug family groupings around him. He imagined their ordered lives, comfortable homes, security. He gave a wry smile. It could all fall apart so quickly, they didn't appreciate that.

Musing on the unfairness of life, a common, insistent theme for Graham, he noticed a small girl on her own talking to a battered teddy bear as she made her way purposefully to the main exit of the bar. He was immediately conscious of the danger for the child who could have been only three or so. He looked around him, trying desperately to identify the child's parents. He quickly realised there were no obvious candidates. The building was so full and the noise level so high it would have been well-nigh impossible to alert others to the child's predicament. He appeared to be the only person who had seen the little one open the door and step outside on to the pavement and beyond, the horribly busy sea front road.

Stricken by thoughts of an imminent catastrophe, Graham pushed himself out of his seat, barging his way through offended drinkers in order to extricate himself and save the child. Once outside, he looked round quickly, spying her just outside the chip shop, seemingly oblivious of anything but her teddy. Breathing a sigh of relief, he jogged up to her. He bent down to look in to her face, placing a hand gently on her shoulder to stop her going any further. 'Hello,' he said, 'what's your name?' The child turned her head reluctantly, took one look at him and burst out crying. This wasn't good, thought Graham. He had hoped to lead her quietly back to the pub but her reaction to him alerted the queue waiting outside the chip shop. A woman in the line, all gold sovereigns and peroxide hair called to her neighbour, 'Hey, look at him, what's he doing? A chorus of disapproval ran through the crowd. A skinny youth in trackie bottoms and a hoody said 'Yeah, he doesn't know her name. He must be trying to run off with her. He's a fucking paedo.'

The little girls' cries grew louder as the adults grew angrier. Graham felt his heart thudding dangerously fast. His hands grew clammy and his stomach roiled. He tried to defend himself but he seemed to have lost the power of speech, a feeble squeak came out of his mouth instead of words. This crowd were definitely not like those in the Sea Horse. They were rough and readier, skinny or gross, their northern accents pronounced and virtually unintelligible to him. He was seized roughly by a man and a woman as, out of the corner of his eye he saw a young woman rush to the child and enfold her in her arms.

She screamed and sobbed wailing, 'Gemma, Gemma, what are you doing out here? What have I told you about wandering off without mummy? Oh, God, you gave me such a fright!' She clutched the child fiercely rendering tiny Gemma hysterical.

Graham made a desperate attempt to break free from his captors and explain his actions to the child's mother, perhaps she would believe him. Not only did he have aggressors at either side of him, however, behind him his way was blocked by a large man covered in tattoos boasting the bulky body of a regular gym and steroid user. 'Where do you think you're going?' he growled, his voice thick with menace. 'We all saw what you were trying to do. I say let's deal with him ourselves. If we get the law involved he'll get off with a slap on the wrist and he'll be round trying it again.'

Graham couldn't believe what was happening to him. He was in the middle of a baying mob more reminiscent of the Middle Ages than 21st Century England. Passers-by had joined the swelling crowd among whom there were pockets of heated discussion as to what should happen to him. Cars were offered to ferry him 'somewhere quiet' for a 'going over.' Castration was mentioned. His captors began dragging him off the pavement and towards the angry sea.

Graham had long since lost his dignity. His jogging bottoms were soaked in urine, fat tears mixed with snot ran down his face, his voice hoarse with desperate protestations. Was this the way his life was going to end?

From somewhere at the back of the crowd a sharp stone was thrown, glancing off Graham's left temple. Blood began to trickle down his face as other stones hit him. Howls erupted from his captors as they, too, were hit. The hands clutching the prisoner's arms loosened as they tried to defend themselves. In the middle of the mayhem, as Graham sunk to the floor unconscious, the sounds of police sirens cut through the air.

Discharged from the Casualty unit of North Tyneside General Hospital later that afternoon, Graham, clutching instructions about warning signs should he feel ill and prescription painkillers, he was taken to North Shields Police Station. The officers ferrying him took no notice of his explanation of events. They were polite and distant. At the station, they led him to a dank, graffiti marked interview room, provided him with a cup of tea and left him to his dismal thoughts for the best part of an hour. Eventually a middle-aged male and younger female entered the room. Graham opened his mouth, ready with his story but was forestalled by the male. 'Let's take this slowly, shall we? Now my name is Detective Bill Tucker and my lovely companion is WPC Shirley Kelly.' The female police officer stiffened at his words, Graham saw her bite her lip, her hands clenched. Detective Tucker, [call me Bill] smiled affably at his captive who got the distinct impression that this was an act he used at every interview, nevertheless his was grateful that the 'bad cop' routine wasn't being employed straightaway at least. Slowly, his interviewers took him through his background before moving to the events of the morning. They paid particular attention to his time in the Sea Horse. Despite trying to prove his innocence regarding his actions, the officers managed to twist everything he said, especially the woman. She looked so biddable but Graham decided she was made of steel. 'So, you expect us to believe that you alerted no one in the Sea Horse about this little girl, made no attempt to find the parents or to talk to the bar manager? Very convenient. You saw a defenceless child on her own and decided that you wanted her for your own perverted reasons. Where were you going to take her? Got a little place tucked away, have you?'

Graham was horrified at this suggestion. He refuted it strongly but his denials sounded feeble even to his ears. He stuttered and stammered, feeling like a rat in a trap. 'Surely someone else in the pub must have seen what happened. I only went after her when she left the premises. I didn't take her outside. I saved her for God's sake.'

The officers shook their heads, clearly cynical about his explanation. Meanwhile, Graham was beside himself. He had no idea how to persuade them to look at events differently. His head hurt, his clothes were a mess and he was truly frightened. 'What can I say to make you believe me? Please help me.' Just then there was a knock at the door of the interview room. A young constable put his head round the door tentatively and said apologetically: 'Sorry to disturb you, there's someone in reception I think you see.' He looked at the irritated faces of his colleagues. 'Honestly, it's

24

important.' The interviewing officers left the room wordlessly leaving Graham sobbing quietly, his head in his hands.

A casually dressed young man, evidently professional from his air of confidence and authority, strode forward to shake the hands of the two officers. Without waiting for them to speak, he said, 'Hello, my name is Rodney Pugh, I'm a solicitor. I understand that you have detained a man in connection with the child who wandered out of the Sea Horse at lunch time?'

'What's it got to do with you, Sir?' Bill Tucker replied curtly. Rodney Pugh was clearly annoyed by Bill Tucker's attitude. 'Well,' he replied, 'You might be interested to know that I'm little Gemma's uncle, I was in the Sea Horse and I saw everything that happened. If you are thinking of charging that man with a criminal offence, it will be a grave injustice. It was clear to me that he was helping.'

'How is that, Sir?' the officer queried, his face masking the distrust he felt. He, along with many of his associates, despised Solicitors for, as they saw it, colluding with criminals they had prosecuted in all good faith. He, nevertheless, indicated a small interviewing room to the left of the main reception area, opening the door and ushering the Solicitor in. When they were sitting, facing each other, he asked the young man to continue his explanation. He did so eagerly: 'Well, Gemma's parents, Pat and Paul, my wife, Catherine and I had arranged to meet for lunch. The Sea Horse was very crowded but we had arrived early and managed to grab a table in the window to the far left of the entrance. We were talking after the meal and Gemma was evidently getting bored. She took her teddy under the table, she decided it was a den. I think we lost track of time and we all assumed she was still down there when I happened to glance out of the window and saw her wander by. I saw your man looking around then following her out while I was desperately trying to push my way through all the drinkers. Gemma must have made her way to the back of the pub and walked around the other side of the bar. You wouldn't have been able to see her from where we were. All of us got out of the Sea Horse as quickly as we could but that ugly scene happened so quickly. That man deserves a medal, not that disgusting behaviour from that mob. It was terrifying!'

Reluctantly, Bill Tucker realised that this version of events was plausible. He sighed, asked Mr Pugh to stay where he was and went to discuss matters with Shirley. She was none too happy. Shaking her head, she said: 'I don't care what anyone says, that bloke is a sex offender, I just know he is. I wouldn't trust him as far as I could throw him.'

'I agree that there's something dodgy about him but this bloke, Pugh's tale rings true. We can't really keep Turner here because we don't trust him. We'd have to build thousands of new cells if we detained everybody we didn't trust!'

Ten minutes later, Graham Turner was standing outside the police station relishing the fresh air, despite the cold, and shaking hands vigorously with his saviour. 'I can't thank you enough for coming to my rescue,' he said. 'I thought they were never going to listen to me. They were going to lock me up and throw away the key!'

'They had nothing,' replied the younger man, 'they would have had to let you go eventually. Now, can I give you a lift somewhere?' He pointed to a small red sports car parked across the road.

'Oh, yes please.' Graham attempted to smile. 'I just want to be home. Whitley Bay, please.'

They were soon on their way, well, thought Graham, on their way somewhere. Although he didn't drive himself, anymore, he was aware that this was not the way to Whitley Bay. 'Erm, where are we going?' he asked his silent driver timorously.

'Somewhere quiet, I thought,' Rodney Pugh replied with a wintery smile. Somewhere I can spend all the time I want with you. It was good luck I saw you today. You probably don't remember me, I was just one of many at St Hugh's. No, I know you don't like girls but boys of 7 or 8, that's a different story, isn't it? You managed to leave teaching by the skin of your teeth because the school governors didn't want a fuss. Well, welcome to your punishment.'

Farewell Avalon

By Jean Laurie

Jean Laurie is inspired to write when an event in the physical world resonates with an emotional experience. She has had several poems and short stories included in anthologies, so she hopes that readers share that emotional response.

The tachograph is ticking. Twenty eight minutes then I've got to stop driving. The M5 is quiet at midnight. Given my quest, it's a blessing there's not much traffic. I turn left onto the A39, signposted Glastonbury, but I'm not going that far. The headlights pick out the old stone milepost, half hidden by ghostly frosted grass. Avalon: three miles.

The refrigerated carrots and raspberries are keeping cool my other cargo. They are bound for London, but the other will be unloaded when I get to my destination. For now I have to use all my concentration to get this thirty two ton artic round the narrow bends leading up the hill. Tree branches brush the windscreen, like witches' fingers trying to grab me through the glass.

At the t-junction there's a break in the dead leaves on the beech hedges and Avalon's neon sign glitters on the summit. I rev the engine and reach the car park just as the tachograph flashes its warning light.

Like most truckers, my cab holds a microwave and kettle, sleeping platform and bedding. Even sleeping in the locked cab I don't feel safe parked up in a layby or out on a deserted industrial estate on the edge of town. Gangs smash the lorry doors and steal the goods. I've had machetes and guns waved at me, warning me to stay in the cab. Although they'd have a shock if they found tonight's cargo. Worse if the police had pulled me over. A body is hard to explain.

I reach over for my duvet jacket and secure the lorry. It's chilly in the May night after the warmth of the cab, but the full moon gives me a good light. The smell of bacon and chips wafts across the forecourt of the transport cafe. The cafe itself is a low brick building, with a prefabricated lean-to attached at the left, where the living quarters are. Beneath the neon sign, in only-slightly smaller letters, shines the legend, 'Arthur Noble - King of the Somerset Sausage'. There's a good few other HGVs at the edge of the car park. I weave through a herd of motorbikes parked close to the door, powerful BMWs and gleaming Kawasakis, and push open the door.

Inside is steamy as a Turkish bath. The place is packed with working truckers who happened to be in the vicinity when the call went out and ex-truckers who ride the highways now as bikers. The youngest are in their fifties, men with paunches poking beyond their black leathers, some with thin grey pony tails, others close shaven. Some have brought their partners, bleached blondes slightly too old for eyeliner, though they wear it anyway. The juke box is playing Jerry Lee Lewis's 'Great Balls of Fire' and a dozen people are jiving near the bay window.

"Lily, good to see you," Clive gives me a suffocating bear hug. He's trucked to Kabul, Cape

Town, Kazakhstan and everywhere between and his face is wrinkled and brown as a walnut.

"Have you got him with you?" he asks anxiously. His breath smells beery. I nod. Clive holds up my hand and yells:

"Hey everybody, this is Lily. I taught her to drive. The first female in Scotland to pass her HGV test. She's brought Arthur home."

Clive doesn't say he also taught me the truckers' code of conduct, that we always help each other out. Especially out of a tight corner. No questions asked. People are shaking my hand or raising their beer bottles and cans to me. Behind the counter, Arthur's half brother and business partner is waiting. Lance looks haggard. He'd rung me last night, hysterical, not quite coherent. Something about the insurance company not paying out and the bank reclaiming the cafe. He grasps my hand between his meaty fingers.

"Thanks Lily, sorry I had to ask you to do this. What can I get you? Healthy options tonight are cannelone or a Greek salad."

"Ok if I order after a shower?" I'm grimy after the drive down from Perth and shower facilities are few and far between for truckers.

"No problem," shouts Lance, over the rising noise of bikers and truckers catching up with each others' news. I give Clive my keys and he heads off to remove Arthur's body from the refrigerated truck. I squeeze through knots of people to reach the calm sanctuary of Arthur's washroom. Bless him, he always wanted us to feel welcome.

When I'm showered and dressed, I walk back into the cafe. Clive and his gang have cleared a space on a

31

table and laid out Arthur. He looks even smaller and stouter lying down. I realise one of his shoes is missing.

"I hope you brought down the witch who killed him," Lance mutters.

"Sorry Lance, she was long gone by the time I reached the hotel." I squeeze his hand. It's still warmly greasy from dishing up sausage sandwiches for the crowd of people gathered to celebrate Arthur's life.

"OK everyone, let the wake begin," yells Clive, punching the jukebox. 'Lovin' Up a Storm' blares around the cafe. Finally, I look at Arthur's face. I haven't dared to since I carried him out of the hotel on a kitchen trolley. I'm startled to see he's smiling his gentle smile. He looks peaceful now, as if the hole in the back of his head doesn't exist anymore. I suddenly have a vision of him sitting up and joining in the jiving. He always was a convivial man.

Lance beckons me over to a quieter table and asks me to tell him everything. I don't hold back, reckoning he'd know if I lied. He winces when I describe the blood-soaked bed.

"Arthur didn't have a criminal record, so I don't think the police will be able to trace him through DNA," Lance says.

"I've told you as much as I know," I say. "Now it's your turn to tell me how the hell Arthur ended up meeting a Russian prostitute in a motorway Hilton in Scotland."

Lance begins to cry. Luckily he has his back to the bikers, who are busy telling each other tales of Arthur's stupendous feats of eating and mad gestures of generosity.

"It's been going on for months," Lance gulps. "He answered an ad on the internet. Vera she's called. She spun him a line about needing to get out of Russia, some story about the Russian mafia. So he agreed to marry her."

Lance pulls out a photograph from his apron pocket. Arthur and a taller bottle-blonde woman wearing a lot of bling are grinning at the camera outside Glastonbury Registry Office. Lance continues,

"Turns out *she* was the Russian mafia. Cleared out his bank account then disappeared last month. You know what Arthur was like. He couldn't believe she was a witch. So he tracked her down. She thought he had more money she could get her hands on. Thought he was a gullible fool, which he was. I told him not to go, I said meet her here. But no."

Lance stops to blow his nose.

"Anyway, he was a bit uneasy about it. Before he left, he gave me a copy of his will. Told me the cafe was mine if anything ever happened to him. Asked me to organise his wake just this way."

"She hit him with something hard, from behind. Maybe she didn't mean to kill him and panicked when he died." I pause to let that sink in.

Lance's face is red and blotched from crying, but he's thinking of me.

"You look dead beat," he says. "You need some sleep before you finish off your delivery."

"The delivery's deadline is tomorrow evening. Right now, I want to give Arthur a send-off to remember."

I grab a bottle of Stella from the table and search out Clive. I want to dance off the adrenalin that's been coursing through my body for the last twelve hours. I lose track of time and place as familiar trucker faces rock and roll past me.

At dawn, Lance unplugs the juke box and calls us to order, Clive and five other bikers lift Arthur onto their shoulders. We process behind as they carry him into the woods at the back of the cafe, carefully picking out the track, all at least a little drunk. Arthur's body is lowered slowly onto the small rowing boat he loved to fish from. Lance dowses it in paraffin and as it's pushed from the shore, he flicks a match into it. The funeral pyre gracefully glides to the deep centre of the lake while the biker guard of honour waits in the glowing light of sunrise. When no more remains of the body or the boat, we head back up the hill. A wave of tiredness hits me and my legs feel very heavy. I crawl into my cab and sleep and sleep through the bright Spring day.

When I wake, it's late afternoon. The frozen veg needs to be delivered by eight p.m. to the Bath branch of Sainsbury's. I reckon I've got time for a bacon sandwich and I definitely need several cups of strong coffee. I step down from the cab into fresh air perfumed with blossom. The forecourt now is completely empty. No BMWs or Yamahas line up like trusty steeds waiting for their riders. No HGVs. No Lance behind the counter and the juke box in the corner a silent tombstone to lost heroes.

I head to the shower room, guessing Lance too is sleeping off last night's excesses. Shrugging off my jeans and t-shirt, I'm aiming to clear off the sweat and salt from last night's jiving, the tunes still echoing in my mind. Then my fuzzy hangover brain registers that the shower's already running and a female voice is singing Dusty's ' Blind Sheep'.

The shower stops running, the curtain swings back and Vera steps out. Even with her yellow hair damply curled and no makeup, I recognise the groomed, statuesque body in the photograph Lance showed me. I don't know which of us is more shocked. She's eyeing the tattoos on my shoulders and back. I feel as unkempt as a schoolgirl in front of the headmistress, waiting for her to pronounce my punishment. She's the first to speak.

"Well well, sweetie. Have you had a good trip down from Perth?" Her voice is accented just enough to be very, very sexy.

"What are you doing here?" I ask. "Where's Lance?"

"Do you think he's lying with a hole in his head too?" She's mocking me. That's exactly the picture in my mind. I can't cope with another bloody body.

"Don't worry," she's saying soothingly. "Lance is just sleeping off a little too much- what you say?- oh, let's say sex."

I can't find words at all and English is my mother tongue. She's reading the shock on my face. Vera turns round and slips into a white satin wrap, all feminine lace.

"Lance knew you'd sort out the body. He says you're such a sentimental softie for all that honour among truckers. Now, we are flying out to Malaga. And you..." She actually pokes me with her immaculately manicured index finger.

"You, little Lily, will drive off to wherever your next delivery is."

"Oh, no I won't." It's hard to think when you're naked and a Russian beauty definitely trumped my sunburnt, muscular arms and tree trunk legs.

"I'll call the police." Even I think this is a feeble threat. Vera laughs.

"And tell them what?" she asks. "That you removed a body from the scene of a crime and illegally disposed of it in the lake? And all your friends will be accomplices too."

She's putting on her gold rings and neck chains.

"I wouldn't linger here too long, sweetie," she advises me. "Avalon is abandoned. Have a nice life."

And she sashays out of the door like Vivien Leigh playing Scarlett O'Hara in 'Gone With The Wind.' I hear her and Lance laughing in the lean-to bedroom.

Finally I pull my jeans and crumpled t-shirt back on and run through the cafe, smashing into red Formica top tables and sending metal chairs clattering to the floor.

Back in the cab, I wipe away my tears with my hand. I reverse the lorry to the far end of the forecourt, then grind it into gear, foot hard on the accelerator. I ram into the side of Avalon, the side where Lance's room is. The thin plaster wall crumples. I have time to see Lance's rolls of fat overlapping the bedsheets and Vera's startled face in the dressing table mirror. Her eyeliner smears down her cheek like a black tear. I keep on going until I reach the far wall, then throw the lorry into reverse. When I'm out from the rubble, Vera lies dead on the fluffy blue rug. Lance staggers to his feet, clutching his chest and fighting to breathe before his heart succumbs to the attack on his heart.

"Farewell Avalon," I salute the neon sign, now lying at an odd angle across the roof, and head back to the mundane M5.

Nothing Rhymes With Ouija

By James Wilson

James Wilson is a digital marketing assistant who enjoys writing a variety of fiction in his free time. His favourite genres are Sci-Fi and Horror. He also enjoys reading, watching films and playing video games.

Knockknockknock.

The board made a dull thud whenever Darren tapped it.

There were five of us. Darren, the group idiot, Katey, the not-quite love of his life, Jamie, the Straight A kid, Susan, or Smoky Suze, and me, Hugo, the greatest kid in the entire world. I may be biased butI remembered a simpler time where tracksuit bottoms and band t-shirts were suitable for a first date.

It began in Darren's attic. We would arrive and he would leave ladies lingerie everywhere as if he had an orgy every night. One prized afternoon, we were chilling out when his mam came bolting up the stairs and screamed that "he should stop taking her underwear from the washing basket". We laughed so hard that fizz came out of our noses.

You may ask why I am telling you this, but what I want you to remember is that Darren was weird.

One day, we were deciding what we should do. Drink was not an option till a few months later when we could drink ourselves silly from a bottle of cheap cider. It was a good time, where fun could be had while sober. We were chattering happily when Darren said lets "talk to the dead", which we batted off as one of his strangesuggestions. He was always getting these insane ideas and we would just go along with them because nobody had the gumption to argue with him.

So, Darren dragged a large locked box out of one of the cupboards. It reminded me of a treasure chest, a mural of a sailing ship painted onto the top. We gathered around it eagerly like if someone had fallen over in the playground. Darren produced a small key from his pocket and slottedit into the lock.

Click.

Darren lifted the lid and we immediately covered our noses. I had only ever smelt something as foul as that one in my life, and that was a rotting sheep I found on a walk years later. The smell of rotting flesh always makes me retch now.

While we were holding our noses like someone had just farted, Darren showed us two things in his "chest of doom". Amongst old toys, he brought out a perfectly clean sheep skull. We knew he was bullshitting but he said that he strangled it, beheaded it and he kept it as a memento. I can never remember if there was a price tag or not. I am sure there was. The second was a folded board. I was excited at first because it looked like Risk or Monopoly but he closed the chest and set it down on the rug.

We didn't realise it was an Ouija Board until he told us (or Squeegee Board as he liked to call it, he couldn't spell it.). When I first saw it I thought it was some weird version of scrabble. The alphabet was displayed in a strange font, with the first ten numbers beneath. Yes and No adorned the top with a strange symbol between them. There were also a small "seeing

40

stone" which reminded me of a droplet of water caused by surface tension. It was perfectly transparent and magnified each letter beneath it. It started over the symbol.

All of us sat down and Darren explained the rules. The stone should never be lifted from the paper or it would break the link and one person would have to sit out and transcribe. Jamie volunteered almost instantly and he sat outside the four person circle, pen poised. Darren explained that if it worked properly, we wouldn't remember what was said so this way someone would verify our conversation. Jamie was trustworthy.

Weprepared ourselves and Darren began, a small raggedy piece of paper in his hand.

"Oh ghosts of the void, please bless us with your presence. We are mortals but we request your council. If you are there, begin the ceremony."

He stared up from the paper and looked at the board like a pirate consulting his map before a clue. We all looked for movement but nothing happened.

"Oh shit, sorry guys I forgot to say, we need to hold hands. Just do what I do." Darren darted for Katey's hand and she reluctantly accepted. I joined my hands with hers and Susan's and she held Darren's. The circle was complete.

My hand kept slipping from Katey's but I held on tight. I can still remember the sweatiness of her hands and the small ripples of fear coming from her.

Darren stared upwards, his eyes shut, like a prisoner embracing the sun's warmth for the first time. We looked at each other nervously and followed, our heads tilted upwards.

Jamie coughed twice then there was silence. It was a long pause because my legs started to ache but I dared not break it in case I died or something (I was gullible at 13 and Darren warned me that I would). The lengthy silence was broken when Darren whispered.

"If you are there, begin the ceremony. We have arrived."

I didn't know what happened but I felt a ripple of energy rush through me from Katey's hand and I directed it into Susan's. It was a like an electric shock but it was warm and didn't make me feel like my veins were straightening suddenly. It happened again and I timed it.

Every 4 seconds, a small shoot of energy would enter from my left hand and leave through my right.

I enjoyed it and the next thing I knew I had an erection. Blood rushed to my cheeks and I tried my best to hide it by moving my legs upwards. "I hope nobody saw" became my single greatest worry for the first half of the session.

"Look!"

I opened my eyes to find Darren staring curiously at the board. I didn't pick up on it at first but then I noticed.

The symbol and seeing stone had moved to the bottom in front of Darren. A small blank space lay between Yes and No now and it was menacing.

"Did you see it move Jamie?" Darren looked at Jamie waiting for the good news that he did.

Darren's smile receded when he saw that Jamie had been doodling on the pad of paper and only looked up to the sound of his name.

"Fucking idiot" Darren ignored Jamie who, when I looked over my shoulder later on, was sniffling.

Darren told us that from now on, once we touch the stone, we couldn't let go till the spirit allowed us. Once again, if you stop touching it, you die and once again, I believed him.

My skin prickled as I placed my fingers on the blob-like dome.

"Good luck guys" Darren smiled. That smile was the sinister smile you always saw before he did something stupid.

My mind wandered and I lost track of time. I checked my watch before we started and it said 6.04pm. I checked again. 11.21pm.

I remember screaming, and then Susan's fingers moving away from the seeing stone. Looking up from the board, I saw they were now clasped to her mouth. I looked at Darren who also withdrew and then Katey until I was the only one left. The stone now had a large crack in the centre.

"Darren, if I move my hands, does it mean I'll die?" I knew it was a stupid question but I really believed.

"No you won't, Susan broke the link so she is the one who is gunna die" Darren cracked a smile in her direction.

All of the blood had drained from her face and was now seeping from the tips of the fingers. It reminded me of a cute video of puppies drinking milk from a glove. He would pour milk down a plastic glove and each one of them would suck on the tips of his fingers.

Susan let out a cry and slapped Darren hard, a thundercrack echoing across the room. She got up and sprinted out leaving her bag, scarf and coat on the couch.

"Ouch" Darren giggled a bit and rubbed the red handprint stained on his face.

"Wait, where is Jamie?" Katey went over to where he was sitting and looked at the notepad. Her eyes traced over the page and she started to laugh.

"What does it say?" Darren pushed past me and sat down next to her.

I followed him and sat on her other side, where I read the hilarity of our session.

It contained a list of words and small phrases we made.

They were as followed:

FOOTBALL

TREE

The list of random words continued until ourcomedic genius started coming through.

PENIS

VAGINA

HUGO

SUCKS

SUSAN

SMELLS

GAY

DARREN

We couldn't turn the page because we were laughing so much but when we finally did, something in the margin drew our attention.

"Wait, what? Jamie left at 8.29pm? Then why does it carry on…"

The second page went as follows:
BRA
JAMIE
MOTHER
FIT

Jamie then wrote down that he was leaving, the time in the margin and a couple of wet patches smudging the writing throughout. I felt kind of bad about it because his mother died a few weeks before.

The odd thing was, the writing continued. The handwriting changing to something neater rather than Jamie's scribbles. It was beautiful.

"My mam must have done it." Darren laughed awkwardly.

"But Darren, she never comes up here" I argued.

"Well she did, I heard her!" He was defiant, and I fell back into line.

"Darren! Say sorry" Katey always scolded him when he was mean to me. She fancied me at the time but I didn't find out till years later.

"Sorry…"

The writing led on for another couple of pages with the same stuff, random words and sometimes sentences thrown in. Even though it was weird, I couldn't help but laugh at DARREN WANKS INTO WATERMELON to which he punched me, hard enough to leave a purple bruise.

Towards the end it got really weird and finally the point where Susan left. SUSAN WILL BE CUT UP AND PUT INTO THE CHEST. 02 APRIL 2011.

We put the paper down and looked at each other. Katey began to cry and proceeded to leave while I stayed. In my 13 year old mind, I needed to help clean up.

I helped Darren put the things back into the chest and in my haste, I told him to burn the pad of paper. I remember he looked at me blankly, before a grin emerged.

"Sure mate, whatever you say".

I only saw Darren a couple of times after that and I moved away to a town nearby as well as schools. I still saw Kateyand Jamie sometimes but it was a rare occasion. When I did, they told me that they didn't hang out with Darren anymore and they hadn't seen Susan since the night of the game. We all assumed she had moved away.

It's funny, whenever I try to picture Susan all I see is the chest.

Aunt Martha

By Harry Gallagher

Harry Gallagher has been writing for much of his life and one day soon hopes to join up the letters. Until then he lives in hope on the coast with a very patient daughter and very small dog.

Hello, yes do come in officer. Such horrible weather today isn't it? Horrible, horrible day, yes. Who? Oh the little girl, yes very sad wasn't it…well I presume she's long gone by now, it's usually the way with these terrible cases isn't it? Long gone, yes. All wrong, having to bury your own. Oh my heart bleeds for them, it really does, and only a year since their little boy too. Did you ever find out what happened to him? No? So sad; such short and tragic lives, some people, yes.

I've considered moving you know, this neighbourhood gets me down and you people can't even keep crime levels down. If it was up to me, I'd bring back hanging. Well, where's the deterrent? Some men have such dark desires don't they?

Sorry? Ah, the little girl, yes. Well, yes, obviously if I hear anything unusual you can be sure I'll be straight onto you officer. No trouble, you can see yourself out, can't you?

Honestly, coming and interrogating an old lady like that!

What's that my dear? Why, I can't hear you if you keep trying to talk in that silly voice, now can I? No,

47

now stop your crying or you'll make Aunt Martha angry again and you wouldn't want that, would you? Yes, I know it's dark but we wouldn't want to hurt your eyes again would we?

Now that was a nice policeman looking for you, but I don't think he'll be bothering an old lady again. Now dear, have you seen your little brother yet? Oh you will do, you will do. All in good time...

Night of the Literary Dead

By James A Tucker

James is a physicist turned Occupational Therapist turned writer. He likes cats, rock music, genre fiction, transpositions and unusual combinations. James also enjoys pedantry about plot and science consistency, even if it's very silly at the same time.

Little does the Faculty of English know the apocalypse that is coming. When there is no more room in the comic store, the geeks shall rise from their bedsits and walk the Earth…

*

The sun was shining as Marcus and Philomena met on their way back to the campus. That was pathetic fallacy but they didn't mind; it was that kind of a day.

'Get any writing done?' Philomena asked him. Marcus noticed she had loosened her floaty pashmina and unbuttoned her cardigan. Which reminded him, he still hadn't written the gratuitous sex scenes for his novel yet. 'Pretty good, I got about six good lines done today,' he said. 'Yourself?'

'I got two whole references written properly into my essay!' she said. 'I was sitting in the park chewing my pen. Very conducive to writing!'

'I went to the Lit and Phil,' boasted Marcus. 'I sneaked down to the Silence Room and I managed to stay there for three whole minutes!'

'Wow!' said Philomena, widening her eyes. 'They say nobody without a PhD has ever lasted more than five!'

'It was hard,' said Marcus modestly, 'but it set me buzzing with poetic energy for hours afterwards.'

They were getting near the campus. Ahead of them was a girl who seemed to have fallen foul of a liquid lunch. She was staggering and weaving left and right, blocking the pavement, and her clothes were disarrayed and ripped. They restricted their pace to avoid running in to her.

'Her friends really shouldn't have abandoned her like that,' said Philomena. 'What are they, Mechanical Engineers?'

'Mech Eng rules!' roared a voice suddenly and hands landed on both their shoulders. Marcus and Philomena jumped, then glared at the tall man who'd come up behind them.

'Kingsley! Don't scare me like that!' protested Philomena.

'Sorry, couldn't resist. Fancy a few bottles of wine in the Union?'

'It's only five o'clock, Kingsley. You sure your method-writing technique will leave your liver intact?'

'It's my wallet I'm worried about. What's that girl doing?'

The woman in front of them had stopped completely. She now seemed to be talking to herself, muttering quietly and indistinctly.

'Do you think she's escaped from the Asylum?' whispered Philomena.

'Let's see,' said Kingsley, and strode forwards. *Confident bastard*, thought Marcus.

'Excuse me,' said Kingsley, 'Are you alright? You look like you—'

The girl lurched around, and time congealed. Her face was twisted, pasty white, red eyed, loose jaw hanging open and spilling ropes of drool and blood down the front of her T-shirt. That shirt bore a slogan that read "Team Edward." Her mouth worked. She seemed to be wearing a huge pair of fake fangs, but through them she groaned 'Blood!' Then with a sudden burst of speed she leapt on Kingsley, sinking her teeth into his neck.

'Aaargh, get her quickly off me!' he screamed, wrestling with her as they staggered back and forth.

'Oh it's horrible,' gasped Philomena, 'a cliché word and an adverb in an ungrammatical sentence construction! Do something!'

Marcus twitched, wary of the clawing savagery ahead of him. The girl was somehow biting and screaming at the same time, a wordless torrent of bestial sound. 'Like what?' Then his inner Neanderthal kicked in. He couldn't pass up a chance to impress a girl. He grabbed his sheets of poetry out of his pocket, rolled them up, ran forward and started whacking the growling girl with them.

Kingsley slumped to the floor, attacker still fastened to his throat. 'Sight... fading...' he gasped. 'Must... tenaciously... hold on...' Philomena rummaged furiously in her bag.

51

The roll of paper in Marcus's hand creased in half with repeated impacts, but the maniac hadn't slowed. 'Bons mots aren't working on her! It's like she just doesn't feel them!' he yelled.

'Try this!' Philomena flung him a huge hardback volume. Marcus caught it and, not without some difficulty, brought it down on the girl's head. She grunted and fell flat and still. The quiet was deafening.

Marcus gingerly reached out and felt the girl's neck. 'She's dead—and she's cold as if she's been dead a while!' he said.

'Kingsley!' said Philomena, desperately rolling the body off their friend. His eyelids fluttered.

'Go… on… without… me,' he gasped, 'happily…' His eyes glazed and a long, slow breath escaped from him.

'It was too late,' said Marcus, 'he'd lost too much taste. I'm sorry.'

'Oh Kingsley,' said Philomena, 'no…' Gingerly, she reached out and gently closed his eyes. Marcus winced, but bad prose was acceptable at the sudden death of a friend.

He stood, aware that the sounds of the city had changed. There was screaming, and yelling. Somewhere there was a huge crash of steel. A pillar of smoke was beginning to rise from the High Street.

'Marcus, what's happening?' Philomena grasped his arm.

Marcus didn't know what to think; whenever he imagined saving girls, he was quite able to deal with the imagined danger. Now, he wasn't so sure. 'I don't know,' he muttered. 'I think we should get to somewhere safe…'

Philomena's grip suddenly tightened as they heard a groan. 'Kingsley! He's still alive!'

Yes, Kingsley was moving. Slowly, mechanically. As Philomena let go, Marcus grabbed her in turn and held her back.

'What are you doing? Let me go, you can't even tell when someone's...' She fell silent as Kingsley sat up. Blood oozed very slowly from the cut in his neck and his eyes were still glazed. His hands, the skin on them now blue and veined, went to his chest. He grabbed the material of his shirt and ripped; below it was another t-shirt, torn, bearing the legend "Doctor Who."

'Oh, Chaucer save me!' groaned Philomena.

Kingsley rose to his feet, moving in clumsy jerks. He reached into his pocket, pulled out a toy plastic device that looked vaguely like the sonic screwdriver on his T-shirt image. He began lurching forwards, holding it out in front of him. The end lit up, making an unconvincing sound effect.

They backed away and turned to run, but shambling around the street corner behind them came two more bloody figures in mutilated Star Trek uniforms. Marcus and Philomena spun around twice, back to back.

'RUN!' screamed a voice and a policeman came charging out of a side alley. He laid into the thing that had been Kingsley, beating him savagely with his truncheon of rolled-up legal documents—but although Kingsley staggered, he did not fall. He poked at the policeman with his Sonic Screwdriver, catching him on the arm.

'The university!' cried Marcus, dragging Philomena past the fight. The policeman managed to knock

53

Kingsley onto the ground and came running away with them.

'What's happening?' gasped Marcus as they stopped just inside the main square.

'It's some kind of new plague!' said the policeman. He was in his thirties, stocky but tall, with a strong-boned face. 'These things can't be stopped by normal words. They attack mindlessly and if they kill you, you turn into a Genre Fan within minutes. It's a massacre out there!'

'Is this the apocalypse?' whimpered Philomena.

'There's no time to terrifyingly worry about that,' said the cop, rubbing his arm where Kingsley had prodded it. 'Oh god—sorry, it just slipped out. Excuse me.'

'It's alright, it's very stressful,' said Marcus. He looked back over his shoulder. Kingsley and the Trekkies were staggering slowly but purposefully after them, and were close to catching up. 'We need to go!'

They ran around the corner, and stopped dead at the horror in front of them.

The university square was carnage. Genre Zombies were everywhere, mouthing senselessly as they lurched after screaming students. They were so tightly packed that there was hardly anywhere for the people to escape. A crowd of creatures wearing wizard robes bundled a struggling man to the ground and started shoving their magic wands up his nose. A monster with a long coat and ridiculously blond hair seized a girl and bit her in the throat.

Some students were fighting back. Homework and newsletters bounced off the creatures on all sides, to no effect. One student on the steps of the Union fired rapid sarcasm at them from a megaphone. He kept shooting put-downs at them, seemingly unable to believe they made no difference, until a zombie with pointed elf-ears started beating him with a rubber nerf sword.

'And I thought I would spend the day just booking adjective junkies,' muttered the policeman.

'The English Faculty,' said Philomena. 'It's our only hope!'

They made the nightmarish run across the edge of the square. The worst of the slaughter was now around the Union, as creatures closed in on the fresh meat of students spilling out of the bar. They dodged a fat zombie in a Thunderbirds shirt to reach the raised walkway—somehow, miraculously clear—and dashed for the end. They were nearly there, and then a creature in a brown coat staggered out to block the end, waving a toy gun.

'Typos!' swore the cop. They turned back—and somehow Kingsley was behind them again.

'Oh no,' groaned Philomena.

Marcus looked at the big book that was still in his hands, and felt a surge of courage. He ran past the cop, and brought the book down hard on the brown coated zombie's head.

It crumpled and lay still.

'You completely killed it!' said the policeman.

Marcus read the title of the book. 'Heavyweight literary criticism to the head. There's only one way to deal with them!'

'There must be more crit in the faculty!' said Philomena.

A groan and a hum of Sonic Screwdriver alerted them to the pursuing Kingsley Zombie. They turned and dashed for their goal, skirting a few more lumbering monstrosities.

At the English Faculty, a mob of zombies in hairy Hobbit feet were hammering on the door. The fugitives stopped, stymied.

Above the zombies, a window opened and a tweed-jacketed figure leaned out, directing an un-mounted projector onto them. The hobbits screamed and ran, text glowing over their skin.

'Get in fast! That won't stop them for long!' cried a voice.

They ran to the doors, opened them with a key card, dived, through. Just as the doors closed, Kingsley crashed into them and started pointing his screwdriver at the lock.

They slumped against the wall, panting for breath.

'Oh poor Kingsley,' said Philomena. 'To be turned into that thing…. oh God, Marcus, do you think some part of him is still alive in there?'

'I don't think so,' Marcus said slowly. 'Real character can't exist in genre fiction, you know that.'

'I—I suppose that's a mercy.'

The tweeded figure appeared at the top of the internal stairs.

'Professor Atwood! Thank goodness!' cried Philomena.

The female professor took off her glasses and rubbed them. 'There's only me left,' she said. 'Everyone else is gone. I managed to clear the building by playing Baudrillard over the tannoy but now the tape's used up.'

Behind them more and more zombies were beating on the doors, which were bending under the sheer weight of the mindless horde. The glass was starting to crack before the T-shirted and costumed multitude.

'We'll make a stand at the reference section on the second floor,' said the professor. 'Come on!'

They forced their legs into motion once more, staggering up the stairs and swinging desks and tables into a makeshift barricade. The professor sorted out piles of the most perspicacious critical essays; they ripped the covers off and started making paper aeroplanes as fast as they could.

A huge crash from below. The undead throng came staggering across the floor, but hit the bottom of the stairs and their numbers choked them. Only a couple abreast could begin climbing.

Marcus flung a dart but only hit an arm. The zombie dropped the action figure it was holding but kept moving. The women folded frantically and handed them to the men, who threw them.

'Ha-ha!' cried the policeman as he scored a direct hit on one wearing a Stormtrooper helmet. As it slumped and rolled down the stairs, a fierce wave of animalistic exultation gripped him.

'Excuse me?' said Marcus.

'What?' The policeman flung another dart.

'Your Point of View just slipped.'

'No it didn't. Absolutely truthfully not.'

'It slipped right onto me!"

'You're making things up paranoidly!' protested the cop.

Marcus recoiled. 'You're infected!'

The policeman stared at him, pale face working soundlessly for a moment, then he flung his head back. 'NOOOOOOOOOOOOOO!'

'He's gone!' cried the professor.

The policeman tore open his jacket to reveal a ripped and bloodied "Game of Thrones" T-shirt. His eyes rolled up white and he pulled a sword-shaped letter opener from a sleeve.

Marcus ducked as the zombie swung a blow over his head. He seized a book from the table and fled backwards.

Philomena flung a dart straight into the cop-zombie's face, but as he crumpled the first of the column reached the barricade and started shoving it aside, apart from one dressed as Spiderman who climbed over. Once again, they ran, down two corridors and took refuge in the professor's room. She slammed the door closed and shut the blinds. On the floor, the body of her erstwhile colleague lay out flat in a Babylon 5 hairstyle.

'Is this the End?' sobbed Philomena. 'Is the only language heard in the world soon to be Klingon?'

'It could be,' said the professor. She was white and shaking. 'If they manage to place a copy of Lord of the Rings on the Book of the Century pedestal, the world will end. It says so in Shakespeare.'

'How did this start?' said Marcus. 'How could the plague get so bad so fast? I thought the threat was contained!'

The professor averted her eyes. 'I have no idea.'

'Wait a moment!' Marcus seized her. 'You're hiding something. I can tell.'

'I didn't know!' screamed Professor Atwood, breaking down. 'It's not my fault! I thought it was literature!'

'What did you do?' screamed Marcus.

'It was 1984,' whispered the Professor. 'I let students read it without protective equipment. It had character, language everything... but... but... it was SCIENCE FICTION ALL ALONG!'

'No,' whispered Marcus, 'What have you done?'

'She dabbled hubristically in Things Man Was Not Meant to Know,' said Philomena.

Marcus turned to face her. She had her hair done up like Princess Leia. He slumped despairingly to his knees as she raised her Lightsaber, and vanished into an abyss of indeterminacy.

Goodboy Gordon

By Harry Gallagher

Harry Gallagher has been writing for much of his life and one day soon hopes to join up the letters. Until then he lives in hope on the coast with a very patient daughter and very small dog.

I am Goodboy Gordon and me the obedientest, happingest, sidepartingly little boyhood in the roader. My mummylet has washinged my cheruby face lost of times today until I am neat neat neat and cleany tidy. And I have done not bad but goody. That is me.

My headly master was is my bester friendman and it was not me sir no sir it was my specially buddy Brian. Bad Brian. Baddy bad Brian. Badlad Brian my mummyness called him today. I love my mummy and she loves her Goodboy Gordon. YES SHE DOES!

But she not likey Brian and he unlike her too three four. He unlike my mummy today very much and my mummy got maddest and ran into Brian bread knife hand. And she not scream nor nothing. She look at Brian in me and I know what she wanting. She wanting Brian out from me and into teacher. Mrs Slimmings. Mrs Slimy Slimmings. She bad lady. Bag lady. Dead lady. And class scream shout run cry.

But is only me. Goodboy Gordon. An' my friendles see me, not Brian. Bad Brian who dun it an' ate lady's eye. And stuck knives in bad childrens. Bad bad bad childrens.

But me Goodboy. Want mummy now…

Where Has Our School Gone?

By Moira Conway

Moira Conway studied for an MA in Creative Writing at Northumbria University. She worked in London as a journalist and magazine Features Writer. Now living in Newcastle, she is part of Victoria Watson's writing group and is working on a collection of short stories. Moira has finished her first novel, *Martha – Maid to the Bronte Sisters*.

As night was falling, children dressed as little Victorians and carrying lanterns made their way through the streets gradually weaving their way towards the school gates like little glow worms, to celebrate their school. This was the end of a day of celebrations remembering all the pupils who had been to the school since it was built. The discussion about what to wear had been going on for weeks. Caps borrowed from grandads, trouser braces dug out from the back of drawers, waistcoats for the boys, dresses and pinafores for the girls, mums had even found bonnets and made mob caps. It was a magnificent display of motherly one-upmanship to get the most authentic-looking Victorian child.

The teachers had come up trumps with pictures of past pupils and events. In pride of place was the black and white slightly faded photograph of the very first pupils which included the great granddad of Tom in Mrs Wilson's class, Year Three, or top class infants as it used to be.

That morning the school had buzzed with excitement as the pupils gathered in the 'big hall' admiring each other's outfits. Miss Dixon, the head teacher, took the final assembly of the year telling them about the people who made the school possible. They learned about the Education Act which said all children would have to go to school. First there had been temporary huts which stood on the field by the terraced houses. Then the huts were replaced with a magnificent Victorian school of red brick, made from the clay in the ground nearby, and a large roof of sleek grey Cumberland slate topped off with little pagoda chimneys. At the end of the school was a smaller building, for the little ones - now called reception - with a square tower with a bell in it which used to ring to tell the children it was time for school. Next to the school, just over the grey stone wall, Miss Dixon told them of the historic St Andrew's cemetery which is over 200 years old with two matching chapels – 'one for Conformists, that's Church of England and one for Non Conformists, which is every other religion'. The children loved looking over the wall at the magnificent trees. In the autumn, they collected the conkers from the massive old horse chestnut. Next to the cemetery, set in large grounds, was a large grey stone building tall with a Gothic tower with Deaf and Dumb Institute 1896 carved into the stone. The Headmistress said it was for children affected by the German Measles which is now preventable by wonderful advances in medicine. The children knew it was now a day school for children with hearing difficulties because they often had sports events together.

When the assembly was over, the children went in single file back to their classrooms.

It was Tom's job to open the classroom door, using two hands to turn the big brass knob and holding it open while everyone passed through. There were already children in the room. They stood around the side of the classroom in silence. Tom went up to a boy and girl standing near his desk.

"Hello!"

They smiled. Others were curious and went up the other visitors, they all smiled but none of them spoke.

"They must be from the Deaf School," said Tom to Katrina, as the teacher clapped her hands for silence and they all sat down. Tom only recognised one boy who looked a bit like him.

After break - or playtime as it was - and a story on the mat, the bell rang for home time and Mrs Wilson reminded them to come back as night fell with lanterns or candles and gather in the yard.

They were winding their way back to school where the visiting children were waiting for them. The school choir started the singing with "When The Boat Comes In" then the rest of the school joined in for a jolly rendition of "The Keel Row". Although the visitors didn't join in the singing, they skipped beside the others when they joined hands as they danced around the school. The boy who looked like Tom stayed beside him and, although they couldn't speak to each other, they had become friends. They stood in from of Miss Dixon in the yard and softly sang a heart-rendering sweet version of "Blown the Wind Southerly" which floated up in the air and wrapped around the school building like a loving blanket. As the parents wiped tears from their eyes, Miss Dixon spoke to the children.

"That was beautiful children; you sounded like a choir of angels. Thank you for celebrating all the boys and girls who came before you. Please go home and take all the happiness of today with you and have a lovely holiday."

Tom walked with his new friend toward the gate in the big stone wall as the visitors left.

Instead of going through the gate, his friend found a foothold in the wall and jumped onto it. With a cheeky grin and a wave, he disappeared over the other side.

As the sun rose over the bell tower and little turrets on the big Cumberland slate roof lorries and cranes came thundering down the street. Negotiating into the school yard they parked by the infants building and went to work.

A wrecking ball was set up and smashed through the roof. The visiting children sat behind the cemetery wall watching silently. A workman noticed them.

"Buzz off, kids this is dangerous."

They all looked sadly at him.

"Nothing to see here kids, off you go."

As he went towards the wall the children bobbed back down.

"Go on, shoo!" He shouted aggressively, trying not to swear.

They all stared at him with tears in their eyes.

"Don't you understand English?"

They didn't move. Another man came to join him. He waved his arms and shouted, he even pretended to climb over the wall. The children started to cry and turned to run away, their Victorian dresses and pinafores blowing in the wind and the boys clutching at their caps. The men watched them run, sobbing and wailing, across the graveyard. They made a terrible blood curdling noise. Seeing their distress and hearing the crying, the workmen began to regret shouting at them. Regret turned to spine chilling fear as a little girl with long golden hair and china white skin stopped on a grave marked by a statue of an angel. Turning her sad face to the men she sighed, slowly faded into the ground, and disappeared.

One by one the other children reached their graves and melted into the ground.

Skull

By Faye Stacey

Faye Stacey is a recently graduated illustration student, she enjoys creating work and writing that focuses on the abstruse or bizarre aspects of life.

No one else could see the skull, see it leering and sneering from the pine fresh foliage. They laughed their haughty laughs and thought it a joke when she finally, meekly, mentioned it.

"A glitter covered skull?" "Surely not?" "Who would put such a thing in a Christmas Tree?" were among the myriad of responses received.

But still it loomed; still it laughed; the glee in the undermining of the mind ostensibly its object. She tried to photograph it and it hid, not moving from its spot, yet refusing to appear on any screen. She brought in the now ancient relic of many years previous, the film camera. And it was an achingly disappointing wait – no skull apparent on the analogue format.

But she could see, see how her colleagues were starting to whisper behind hands and magazines, and worry for her and her fixation on the thing that wasn't there.

The caustic stare of the skull dissolved her soul as she sat at her desk. Until, one afternoon, when the building was quiet, she knelt beside its hiding place, shifted the branches aside and placed a hand on the rough crown of the glittered abomination and was inexorably wiped from existence. Not a noise or a squeak; just the mottled surface under the palm and then the air in the space where she ought to have been.

The skull rejoiced, its work complete, and moved on to discover who the next object of corruption would be.

The Chocolatier

By Kay Stewart

Kay Stewart is a North-East-based PR consultant, married with two teenagers, loves stand up comedy, running and writing. Sounds like a strange combination but it works for her!

His sweat smelt of cat piss and his feet of mouldy bacon. The flat was not much better with the sour aroma exploding out of the door when it opened. But his hands, ah, his hands, they were soft and delicious. They were fragrant with scents of vanilla, cocoa from foreign lands and fresh creamy fudge from the years of chocolate making. People wanted to kiss those beautiful fingers all the time, tempted to gobble them up and sell their soul to this mysterious devil on the 13th floor.

Young, beautiful girls with swishy perfumed hair swept past Mrs Reuben's apartment, upwards and upwards, drawn by the sweet allure of the 13th floor. Sometimes she thought she could actually see their scent, like fragile wisps of autumnal smoke gently following them, or ephemeral bridesmaids gliding over the stained corridors.

If she sat very quietly, hardly breathing, she could just make out their timid knocking. It was always one, two, three beats before his heavy key turned and the hinges grated loudly.

A nervous laugh. And then another.

They never came down. Those delicate sweet-toothed maidens opened the dark door to their inner-most souls and found their rounded bellies splitting with ganache, rich butters, pralines and kirsch-filled truffles. Those most exquisite chocolates just dissolved on their tongues. One brief second of rapture, eyes closed, breathing still, held in for a moment, to savour every last thing and then they were gone.

Their expensive smells of Chanel and Miss Dior became fainter and fainter, falling onto the corridor's linoleum and trampled by work boots, battered leather brogues, tiny stilettos and worn nylon slippers.

A scratchy recording of Glen Miller's *In the Mood* began and Mrs Reubens sensed him swaying, dancing, alone again.

Hello, Linda

By Andrew Atkinson

Andrew Atkinson has been writing for six years, mostly sci-fi and fantasy but the occasional horror, and has had several short stories published. He lives in Newcastle with his partner and two children.

When the phone rang it filled Linda with dread. It would be Jim, like it was the last time, and every time the phone had rang for the last two days. But she knew it couldn't be Jim: Jim was dead. Slowly she reached out a trembling hand and picked up the receiver.

"Hello, Linda." Jim's voice emanated from the phone.

Linda screamed and slammed the phone down. How could he be phoning her? She had killed him.

She had brought the hammer down on her husband's head. He'd staggered backwards, stunned. Linda pressed home her attack and had brought the hammer down a second and third time. She'd raised the hammer for a fourth blow, but stopped when Jim finally fell to the floor, blood flowing freely from the wounds on his scalp.

She'd dropped the hammer and ran for the bathroom, choking back the vomit that was trying to fight its way out of her stomach. She couldn't hold it down for long and was just able to lift up the toilet seat before she threw up violently.

When it was clear she had finished vomiting, Linda had forced herself to calm down and look at her reflection in the mirror. He'd had it coming, she knew that. He had told her he was going to leave her, and for a girl half his age. The humiliation she had felt was unbearable. At first she had pretended to be resigned to the fact, that it had come as no surprise, but secretly she was bubbling with anger and hurt pride. He had said he was going to pack his suitcase, and that was when Linda had noticed the hammer lying on the coffee table. She'd been using it to put up pictures of her and Jim's wedding just an hour ago and hadn't got round to putting it away. Before she had time to think about it she snatched up the hammer and smacked it down on her husband's head. That would teach him for treating her like shit. The full force of what she had done hit her as Jim lay dead on the living room floor, blood spreading over the cream carpet.

She'd known she had to get rid of the body, so she had waited until after dark and had dragged the body out to Jim's tool shed. She knew he had a chainsaw in there, and would often be in there working away on something when normal people would be in bed, so the noise wouldn't attract attention.

Several times she'd had to stop dismembering Jim's body to throw up in the corner, dimly thinking she would have to clean that up as well as everything else. Finally she thought she'd got him to the right size to stuff into their suitcases. She'd gone inside and took the suitcases out to the shed; carefully arranging the body parts in them so there was no way they could fall out. Then she had hurried inside, changed her clothes, and stuffed the bloodstained dress she had been wearing inside one of the suitcases.

74

After she had packed the suitcases into the boot of her car, along with Jim's spade, she had gone back inside and stared at the pool of blood on the living room carpet. She didn't know how long she had been standing there before she realised the carpet would have to be replaced. She had almost laughed when she realised she would struggle to remove it without Jim's help, but an hour later she had managed to roll up the carpet and force it onto the back seat of the car.

Then she'd driven out to the nearby woods and buried the suitcases and carpet in as deep a grave as she could dig...

...the phone rang again. Linda stared wide-eyed as the ringing seemed to get louder and louder. She screamed and put her hand over her ears, the ringing just got louder and louder until she thought her ears were going to explode with the effort of trying not to hear.

It stopped abruptly. The answer machine had kicked in. After the answer message had been played there was a click and then silence. But the machine showed there was one message. Shaking with fear Linda reached out and pressed the play button.

"Hello, Linda."

She screamed again and wrenched the phone out of the wall, and then threw it with all of her strength, the phone crashed into the wall and smashed to pieces. Crying, she sank back into her chair. She thought she must be going mad. There was no way Jim could be phoning her, she knew that. But there was no mistaking that voice.

She jumped when her mobile phone started to ring. Taking a deep breath she answered her phone.

"Hello, Linda," she was about to throw the phone away when the voice went on "Linda? Are you there?"

"Carol?"

"Jesus, Linda, what's the matter with you? I've been phoning you for the last two days; every time you answer you just hang up again."

"Two days?" Linda replied weekly. Was it possible she had imagined the whole thing? She tried to suppress a giggle as her sister continued.

"I'm phoning from the airport," Carol said "I got here as quickly as I could. You wouldn't believe how hard it is to get a last minute flight from New Zealand."

"You're in London?" Linda had to hold off her instinct to panic; telling herself it was OK, there was no reason for Carol to suspect her of anything.

"You're damn right I'm in London, I'll be at you place as soon as possible. Unless you want to send that lovely husband of yours to come and pick me up?"

"Jim's out of town," Linda said "Won't be back for a few days." She was amazed at how easily the lie came to her.

"Is that why you sound so weird?" Carol asked "Missing your loved one?"

"Something like that," Linda said with a nervous laugh.

"Well anyway," Carol said "I'll be there soon, and you can tell me what's got into you these last couple of days."

"OK, bye." Linda hung up without waiting to hear Carol's reply. It had all been her imagination. She started to laugh. Jim was out of her life for good, she had got away with murder, she had no idea it could be so easy. Carol was coming to visit and Linda would cry on her shoulder about how Jim had left her and gone off with his fancy woman. She would say she had no idea where, but wasn't it just as well they didn't have kids?

Linda went into the bathroom and started creating the image of the betrayed wife. She put her make-up on and then poked herself in the eyes, her eyes watered and her make-up ran. Now when Carol arrived Linda would look like she had been crying. Then she ran to the bedroom and started tearing all of Jim's clothes to shreds, using a pair of scissors on the tougher material. Then she ran into the living room and threw every photo of her and Jim to the floor, smashing the glass in the frames, the fact she hadn't slept for two days completed the image nicely.

She had only just finished with the last photo when the doorbell rang. Linda took one last look at herself in the mirror. She didn't look much like a woman whose husband had just left her, she had to fight back the urge to giggle, force herself to look sad, but other than that there wasn't much else she could do.

The doorbell rang again and Linda slowly went to open the door. Going too fast would make her look happy, she decided. When she opened the door she found herself staring at a tall man, he was standing in the shadows so she couldn't make out any facial features, but she decided it must be Carol's taxi driver. She leaned around him to see if Carol was coming up the path behind him. When she saw the path was empty she looked back up at the man. He stepped into the light and Linda saw his face for the first time; an icy feeling ran down her spine, fear filled her face and she stumbled backwards, knocking a vase of flowers off the small table next to the living room door.

As the man shuffled forwards, Linda kept backing away until she was trapped in the corner of the room. Linda opened her mouth and screamed.

"Hello, Linda." Jim rasped as his decaying hands wrapped around her throat.

Hangman

By Allison Davies

Alli is a writer based in Northumberland, UK. She's a graduate of Northumbria University's MA in Creative Writing where she went to finish a novel and ended up writing a screenplay. She now writes mostly for theatre.

Stand at the front door. Peer through frosted glass. Fuzzy outlines pass outside as people hurry along the pavement. Reach for the handle. Go on. Reach. Imagine the feel of cool, smooth metal.

And I almost make it; imagine pressing down, the click as the latch disengages, the feeling of sunlight on my face as I step into the garden. My throat constricts and I feel the fear build as the scars on my wrist begin to burn.

I used to be different. Happy, confident, afraid of nothing, that's what my friends would say. I went out all the time. It's normal. Every day without thinking you walk the dog, pop to the shops, go to work, out for a drink, whatever. It's what people do.

It's what I did.

Not anymore. I haven't seen my friends for weeks. They probably think I'm still on leave, enjoying sangria and Spanish sunshine. And I can't call them, or even send an email. I tried and the punishment came quickly.

I know what you're think. She's barking, got a screw loose, a few sequins short of a ball gown, and perhaps you're right. Maybe it's all in my head. But what if it's not?

It started with the phone call. That first night I was exhausted and looking forward to at least eleven hours under the duvet. I'd just finished the design work on the Towers building, a splinter of glass and chrome set to be the tallest in that part of the city. My team and I had put in months of early starts and late finishes. Leaving the office before 9 or 10 pm was a rarity, so we were all wrung out and ready for a break before the next project kicked off. I'd planned a trip to Barcelona, but first I wanted to go home, lock the world outside, climb into bed and tumble into deep, luxuriant sleep.

And I did right until the sound of the ringtone seeped into my brain, waking me at 3.03 am. "What?" I said as I flipped on the bedside light, pressed the answer key and waited for my mother's inevitable, "I'm sorry, have I got the time wrong again?"

I imagined her pacing the terrace of her Singapore apartment. She's old and forgetful and sometimes I'm not kind to her. "What's the matter this time, Mum? It's 3 am. "I was sleeping"

No reply. Not my mother after all. A wrong number then.

I was about to hang up when I heard it: hard to make out, almost but not quite like breathing, and a definite sense that there was someone on the other end of the call.

Even modern technology occasionally gives up the ghost during the wet season so I waited. The sound came again, clearer this time, more distinct. Not breathing.

Scratching; the sound a bird makes when it's trapped up a chimney.

Maybe Mum had fallen and couldn't speak. "It's OK. Don't worry. I'll call Mr Yu."

Again the noise came, louder this time.

It was cold. My breath flared out in the puddle of light surrounding the bedside table. I shivered and pulled the duvet up around my shoulders. I should have altered the heating before I came upstairs. The noise came again and I felt my skin contract as tiny hairs rose on the back of my neck. It was definitely scratching, as if someone was dragging their finger nails along a metal surface, and it wasn't coming from the phone.

Scrape; somewhere close, scrape scrape; somewhere closer. Scrape, scrape, scrape. It was coming from inside my bedroom, frantic now, as if an animal was scrabbling to free itself from a trap. It was here, with me, somewhere out of sight at the foot of my bed. I was still clutching the handset. As I dropped it, the light bulb shattered, plunging the room into darkness.

My stomach roiled. My hands clenched, so tightly I felt the sting as each of my carefully manicured finger nails broke through the surface of my palms. As the scratching built to a crescendo I could barely breathe. Cold sweat drenched my t-shirt.

The fear flooding every synapse was deep and visceral as I was bathed in a torrent of pure malevolence. Wave after wave, cold terror, buffeting from every side until I felt like I was teetering on the edge of a precipice and about to fall. Just as I felt myself tip forward, something brushed my throat, the lightest of touches, soft fingertips at the base of my throat.

There was a splintered crash as the glass on my bedside table flew across the room and smashed against the door. The scratching stopped abruptly. A crushing, weight settled on my chest and the pressure on my throat grew stronger. An invisible force pinned me to the bed. I panicked, thrashed my legs, tried to break free, and blacked out.

When I came to I didn't dare move, but lay sprawled across the bed, scanning the night, listening for the smallest sound. Eventually I sank into restless, fragmented sleep and woke at dawn with an aching throat and a bedroom floor littered with tiny shards of glass. Not stopping to clear them up, I stuffed a few clothes into a backpack, grabbed my passport and left for the airport.

Barcelona was wonderful and after five days of sunshine, Gaudi and tapas, I'd almost persuaded myself it was a nightmare, or some kind of psychosis brought on by over-tiredness. My trip was uneventful, apart from on the last evening. I stayed up late talking and drinking with friends I'd made at the hotel and had the odd sense that someone was watching me, yet when I turned around, there was just a blank wall a few metres behind me. As I made my way upstairs to bed, the feeling persisted. I had a shower, felt much better and glanced out of the window to enjoy the lights one last time.

There was a man on the street outside. He was small, and despite the heat wore a thick overcoat and a hat pulled low on his brow. There was something odd about his posture. His shoulders were raised and his back hunched as if his upper spine was malformed. One by one the street lamps flickered and went out until there was a single patch of illuminated pavement where he stood. My stomach knotted. He tilted his chin, looked up and for a few moments our eyes met. There was deep, bitter hatred in his stare, yet I could not break away. The final street light blinked out and there was a cracking sound as the mirror fractured above the dressing table.

I recoiled, snapped the curtains shut and waited for my pulse to slow. When I peered out a few moments later the street looked perfectly normal, bathed in the sodium flare of a thousand city lights. There was no sign of my stalker. A waking dream brought on my too much rioja and sun I decided and managed to maintain the illusion all the way home, until the taxi dropped me off outside my door.

I turned the key in the lock. Inside the hall, the floor was littered with broken glass. It seemed every mirror in the house had been dashed to the ground; every wine glass, vase and tumbler lay smashed at the bottom of the stairs. As the light streamed in on that September evening, the sight of so many tiny, refracted sunsets was beautiful. Almost.

It was almost dark by the time I'd cleared up. I wrapped the last remnants of my favourite antique mirror in newspaper and felt a sharp, stabbing pain from where a shard of glass cut deep into my wrist. The wound bled heavily and though I did all the stuff you're supposed to, elevating the limb and applying pressure, it took a long time for the flow to stop. Too long. I crawled into bed feeling weak and sick and desperately afraid of what was to come.

When my phone rang at 3.03am I thought my heart would fly out of my chest.

83

The scenario played out exactly as before. First the scraping sound, getting closer and closer, the sense of evil building, the terror as the noise grew louder. As the light bulb blew and I felt those fingers close around my throat I was sure this time I would die.

I came to with a burning throat and bloodstains on the sheets where my wrist had bled in the night. Using my phone as a mirror I checked my neck. Ten ovals stained my skin purple. I knew exactly who'd made them.

It's happened every night since. Why can't I leave? Why don't I call and tell someone? Because I get the feeling that it doesn't end here. That the attacking force is attached to me and not just this building; that if I involve someone else I'll infect them somehow. He followed me to Barcelona, so I know there's no escape, that where ever I go he'll track me.

I won't let him win. Yesterday I found a coil of rope tucked behind a pile of packing cases in the attic. It's old, but strong enough to do the job. I'll decide when the time is right, and then...

It's my own fault. I didn't listen when my mother told me not to buy the house. Her Chinese superstitions drive me crazy. She warned me that the diào sǐ guǐ, the ghost they call the hangman, would come, would bind himself to me and give me no rest, but I loved the high ceilings, large windows and the deep, light stairwell, and I got the place cheap.

"It's a bad house. Don't buy it." she said.

"Mum. This is Newcastle. It's 2013. You know I don't believe in those old stories."

"It's bad luck. Very bad. I worry for you. " But as usual, I ignored her.

When I moved in the house had been empty for almost three years so there was a bit of work to do, but once the walls were freshly painted, the new kitchen in and the broken woodwork on the landing replaced, I forgot about the last owner, the unhappy, tormented man from Shanghai who slashed his wrists with a blade of glass from a broken mirror, took a length of rope and hung himself from the banister in the early hours one September night.

Poetry

By Harry Gallagher

Harry Gallagher has been writing for much of his life and one day soon hopes to join up the letters. Until then he lives in hope on the coast with a very patient daughter and very small dog.

Gothika Black

Gothika Black, tattooed princess
Dressed to attract the darkness
Which lives in the nightmares
Of abandoned children everywhere

She wears only black
Black boots, black dress
Black coat, black hat
Black tights, black eyes
Black and blue heart

Freshly minted razor marks
Point the way in memorium
Of what happened last time
She dressed for the sun

But try as she might
The switch stays off
And will not be reached
By the little girl
In the summer dress
Sitting crying in the darkness.

Queen of Nocturne

She is by nature feline
The Queen of Nocturne
A slinky skulker
Ever seeking shade

Only breaking cover
To eversobriefly bask
In the adoring arms
Of the sun
Before retiring back
To padded shadow

Sometimes she crosses my path
Lighting up my surrounds as she comes
Sometimes I can almost touch her
Sometimes she brushes against me
Almost imperceptibly
Leaving me afloat
On nimbus number nine…

River Hag

Coal black deep
Cold breathless sleep
Snatching waiting
Impatient hating
The warmth of a lover
So squeezes another

Drop of despair
As the terminal air
Departs from lung
The cut out is hung
Like a mannequin on reeds
And as death breathes
Her icy nails
Turn skin to scales
And grip and grip and grip.

Dead Bad Haiku

On Heaven's seabed
Cherubim and Heroin
Lifeless blue angels.

Siren

In eighteen hundred and eighty one
Just into New Year's Day
An icy howl wound around
The old lighthouse in Whitley Bay

Where a distance from the revelry
The keeper kept his eyes
Upon the rocks beneath him
And checked the swell for size

With the passing of the old year
Not yet a minute old
The keeper looked upon a sight
That ran his blood to cold

For dancing in the window
Up on the lighthouse top
Was the figure of an angel
Defying the hundred foot drop

Dressed in rags that radiated
Beams of bright white light
She sang in pure magnetic tones
That warmed a New Year's night

She held his gaze for what seemed like days
And then she held his breath
As he climbed out of the window
And stepped out to his death

•

In eighteen hundred and eighty one
Just into New Year's Day
Time froze in the lighthouse
Forever in Whitley Bay

And the calendar upon the wall
Inside the lighthouse dome
Will now forever read
The perfect palindrome -
1881.

My Witch

In the blue black night
White hot gas giants

Give way to the sight
Of a girl made from quicksilver

It is my witch
Flying in from the ether
For an irregular date
With her over-familiar

And for the shortest while
I'll have her on my arm
Before this charm in a skin
Will wing her way
Away

She has need of
Neither hat nor broom
A sonic boom greets
My mistress of mercury
Equipped with a me shaped key
Shape shifting intermittently
Whispering, "Now you see me..."

All Saints

All saints and all souls gathered
On All Hallows' Eve
With today's lesson in superstition
Led by a very modern Father Steve

Smashing up the brimstone
Extinguishing the fire

Welcoming the gambler
The robber and the liar

No hell or fury or damnation
No forbidden fruits of Eve
Only modern gospels count
In the lovely church of Steve

Cycling down country lanes
Recycling "Pause for thought"s
Riding wild with boys of ten
In their grey school shorts

Singing modern Christian songs
Strumming his guitar
Wrestling with unholy thoughts
And "Thou shalt not"s imposed from afar

And the longer the need lingers
The firmer he represses
But he can't control his fingers
As he mentally undresses

And the sermon today dedicated to
The father, son and Holy Ghost
Should focus on what happens to men
When celibacy's imposed.

Snouty

The boy from number 3 Hall Close
Got called Snouty on account of his nose

Rhyming rose tinted memories
On the cruelty of childhood
The uncomfortable details erased
Such as the tears that burned his face
And Snouty how do you spell 'bullied'?

Now the man turns up on Facebook
Damaged and world wary
His father having carried on the work
Kicked off by his peers
His fears realised
As his daddy's eyes
Poured malice down like rain
The pain accumulated
He married the first girl he dated
And as slow and as sure as spite
He became his own father

Face set in stone
With a roman nose
To glare down from
And his heavy hands
And brick blunt wit
And his vicious mouth
And his mean old tongue
Snarling 'pass it on, pass it on'…

The Visit

By Victoria Watson

Victoria Watson is a proofreader, Creative Writing tutor and author. She is the official blogger for Whitley Bay Film Festival and currently runs two weekly writing groups.

It's not my first visit here; I've been a few times before. I've often wondered about the semantics of it all: can it be a visit when, at first, I was summoned?

Stupid girls, playing with things they don't understand, I thought to myself as I moved the glass around the makeshift board. I glanced at their faces, initially unsure if it was delight or fear dancing across their candlelit features. One of the teenage girls was going bright red, blinking rapidly as the glass danced from letter to letter. Another absent-mindedly picked at a white-headed on her chin. Was the ginger one going to cry? Her blue eyes were filling with tears.

D-O-N-T-I-N-V-I-T-E-A-V-I-S-I-T-I-F-Y-O-U-C-A-N-T-H-A-N-D-L-E-I-T

A lone tear trickled down the cheek of the red-head. Spotty face lowered her eyes; she'd taken her fingers off the glass. Four fingers rested on the glass now, trembling. I wondered what they'd expected to see – a headless woman in a nightgown? A highwayman? Ghostly Victorian children? If there was the ability to bet in this world, I could have won handsomely. I knew they'd never expected to see me. Then again, I suspect they hadn't really expected the board to work. They'd watched one too many movies at their sleepover and thought it'd be a laugh – a kind of rite of passage.

I thought back to my own teenage days – had I ever done this? These kids didn't look as wild as I had been. If only my teens had been spent in friends' bedrooms – not down the park dropping acid with God knows who. This lot looked about thirteen, that was when it had all started to go wrong for me.

D-O-Y-O-U-W-A-N-T-T-O-S-E-E-M-E

'No!' Shrieked the one with the braces.

H-A-H-A

I wanted to scare them, make them realise that all actions have consequences. Braces blew out the candle, as it that would stop me.

I-A-M-S-T-I-L-L-H-E-R-E

No-one could see it in the darkness.

'The glass, it's still moving,' whispered the acne-ridden one.

'Shut up Courtney,' snapped braces. Ginger remained silent, crying without making a sound.

I'd like to absolve myself of responsibility by blaming everything on Tom Pyburn but I knew I had to accept that I'd been my own undoing. The more I thought about it, the more angry I became. And I'd had a long time to think about it.

I flipped the board and launched the glass across the room. It shattered on hitting the wall. The trio screamed – what good did they think *that* would do? They huddled together, shuffling their bums across the room until they reached the corner. That temporarily brightened my mood, I laughed. The vintage lamp flickered. That had nothing to do with me but its effect made me smile. The girls, all sobbing now, appeared unable to move.

I shouted as loud as I could but my message reached their ears as a whisper.

'That wasn't me, but this is.' With all my might, I concentrated on making myself visible. Ginger took one look at my ghostly outline and promptly fainted without fuss or noise. The other two stared, wide-eyed and open-mouthed. Braces seemed unconcerned at the stream of mucus running from her nose. Spotty blinked rapidly. They breathed in unison, shallow and frequent but each seemed entirely unaware of the others presence, they were so focussed on the apparition. Although they seemed terrified, I had to admit I was somewhat disappointed. They didn't seem frightened, or even surprised, by the way I looked.

I glanced down to check, everything was as I expected. Track mark upon track mark, ligature marks around my neck. My emaciated figure made no difference whatsoever.

That was my first visit but since then I've visited often. Once that door had been opened, there was no way of closing it. I think of spotty and her friends, snivelling as they sunk the blades into their veins, the blood flowing into the carpet the same way a fizzy drink had earlier in the evening. I felt buoyed having reduced them from innocents to corpses in just a couple of hours. I had considered leaving a bloody message on the wall but I decided it was just too clichéd, although I had been amused at the thought of a wild goose chase, the police looking for a murderer. No, I was content to be the unseen, unknown puppet master. I enjoyed the control and realised before the girls were even cold that I was not willing to relinquish it.

I took pleasure in the blood curdling screams from spotty's mother, revelled in the arguments and accusations when the estranged father finally appeared. Raised voices, sobs, screams.

And then came the police photographer. I really liked him. I toyed with him, partially appearing in photos but not in the next. An object moved, replaced – confusing him. I whispered in his ear, lightly brushing his neck, leaving him confused. It was almost too easy. Almost.

He was working late, determined to finish off his shots before leaving, unwilling to have the scene disrupted further. A couple of whispers and he was mine.

When the father found him hanging there, there was no screaming or shouting, it was all very calm and quiet. He picked up one of the blades, wondering if it was the one his daughter had used only hours earlier, and drew it across his throat in one swift motion.

I knew I wouldn't have to even push the mother, I just left her to her own devices and, sure enough, the pills and booze soon finished the job.

I like having the place to myself but I'm really looking forward to meeting the new occupants…

If you enjoyed this anthology please consider other titles by Wild Wolf Publishing, including:

Wild Wolf's Twisted Tails

Holiday of the Dead

Unlikely Killer

Sinema: The Northumberland Massacre

11:59

I'd Sooner Starve

Myra, Beyond Saddleworth

The Adventures of Charlie Smithers

Lightning Source UK Ltd.
Milton Keynes UK
UKOW02f0641010215

245414UK00002B/42/P